THE SUPER SECRET ADVENTURE CLUB

by George McClements

SCHOLASTIC

New York Toronto London Auckland
Sydney Mexico City New Delhi Hong Kong

ISBN 978-0-545-43685-4

12 11 10 9 8 7 6 5 4 3 2 1   12 13 14 15 16 17/0

Printed in the U.S.A.   40
First printing, September 2012

That's **MY** flag, Sam!

No, it's not, Bea.
Mom gave it to me.

Super

Keep out
Bea!

Now we have
to name it.

It's a

Rocket,

so we'll call it . . .

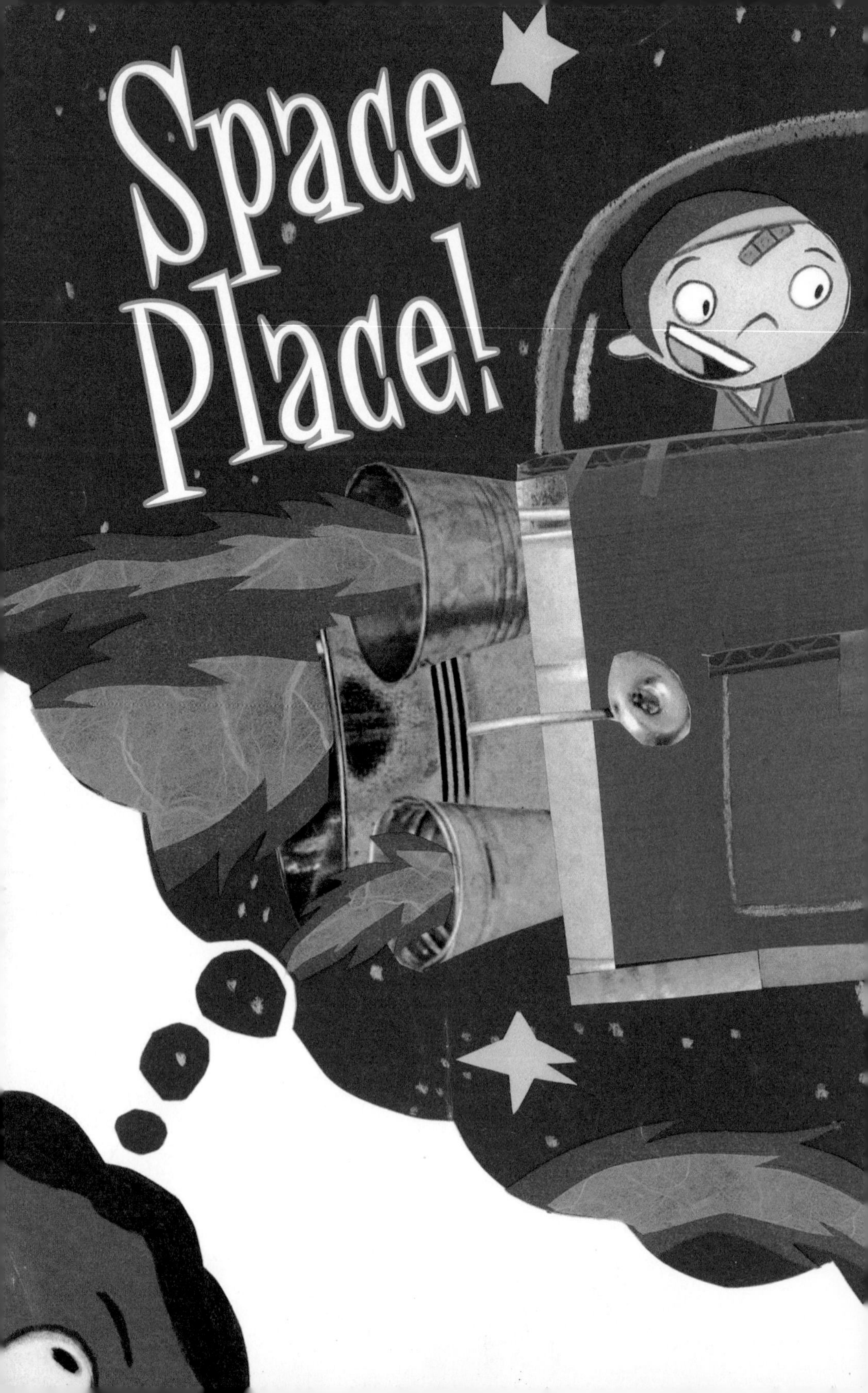
Space Place!

It's **not** a rocket, Matt.
Look closer and you'll see . . .

It's a **T-Rex!**

We'll call
it our
Dinosaur
Den!

Hold on!

It's **not** a T-Rex, Luke.

It's a
Pirate
Ship!

We'll call it the

PIRATE PORT.

No!

Pirate Ship!

T-Rex!
Rocket!

Will you boys stop yelling about your

Super Secret

adventure

Clubhouse?

That's it!

It's perfect!

Welcome to

THE SUPER SECRET
ADVENTURE CLUB
Danger
Keep out Bea!
Beware
This side up